HOME IN THE CAVE

BY JANET HALFMANN
ILLUSTRATED BY SHENNEN BERSANI

On a ceiling deep within a cave, Baby Bat held tight to his mom. Thousands of other moms and babies crowded close, looking like a furry blanket.

In the blackness, Baby Bat filled his tummy with warm milk. He heard squeaking and chirping all around him. The pup felt warm, cozy, and at home in the bat nursery.

I love this cave, he thought. *I never want to leave it. Never!*

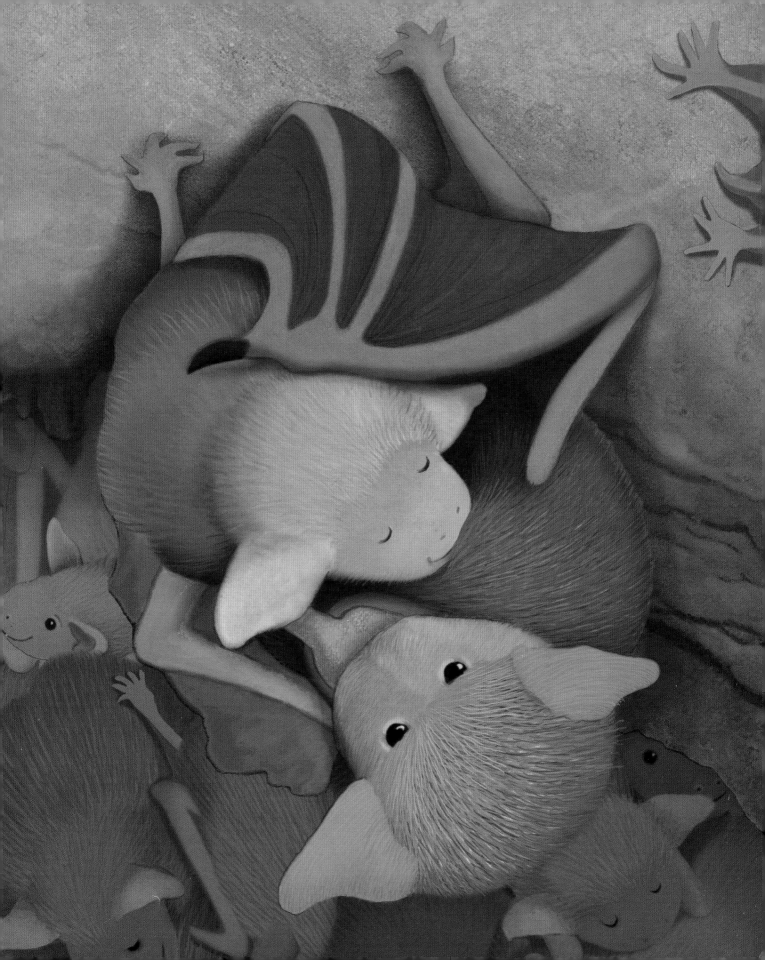

Soon it was dusk and time for the mother bats to leave the cave to hunt insects.

"Remember to practice flapping your wings," said Mom. "You're almost old enough to hunt with me."

Then she was off, in a roar of thousands of flapping wings. The bats zoomed around stalactites hanging from the ceiling like icicles. They soared past stalagmites poking up from the floor like sand castles.

Baby Bat didn't like his mom to go away, and he didn't want to practice flapping his wings. He figured that if he didn't learn to fly, he'd never have to leave the cave.

To make the night go faster, the little bats told stories:

"Last night, my mom caught a gazillion mayflies."

"My mom ate a moth bigger than this room!"

"My mom almost got snatched by an owl."

"That's nothing. My mom flew right between a fox's sharp teeth!"

Owls, foxes with sharp teeth? Now Baby Bat was even more certain that he never wanted to leave the cave. He hid under his wing, wishing his mom would come home soon.

He heard flapping wings and stuck out his head. But instead of his mom, he found the little bats exercising their wings.

Baby Bat knew that his mom would ask if he had practiced, so he flapped his wings *veerrrrry* slowly. His mind was still on owls and foxes, and without realizing it . . . his toes let go of the ceiling.

He was flying! He tried to use his sonar to tell him where he was going, but . . .

. . . thud! He crashed into a wall. Down he fell, smack into a messy nest on a ledge.

When he opened his eyes, a whiskery face touched his own.

"Hi there, I'm Pluribus Packrat," said the whiskery face. "Are you okay?"

"I think so," said Baby Bat, "but why is your nest so lumpy?"

Oh, that's just the shiny trinkets I've collected. These coins say *E PLURIBUS UNUM*. That's where I got my name.

"Hey, I was just about to go exploring . . . want to come along? We can use my flashlight and follow the scent trails I've made from room to room."

Near the entrance, the pair woke a phoebe nesting on a ledge.

In the leaves below, Pluribus almost stepped on a rattlesnake. Its rattle echoed through the cave: *raatttlllle . . . raaaattttlllllle.*

A little further inside, bright-orange cave salamanders darted across damp walls.

Plop! A cave cricket jumped onto Pluribus. Its extra-long feelers waved about. Pluribus shook the cricket off and it scurried away.

Deep in the cave, the pair visited Baby Bat's nursery. Pluribus jumped onto a ledge just above a huge pile of bat droppings, called guano, covering the floor.

"I know you love this room," said Pluribus, "but thousands of other animals love it, too. And they love it because of you and the rest of the bats."

"Because of me?" asked Baby Bat.

"Bats are very important to caves," explained Pluribus. "All the food in a cave comes from outside, and bats bring in most of it. They fly out to catch insects, and then turn them into droppings for other cave critters to eat."

The smelly guano swarmed with thousands of critters—springtails, mites, beetles, flies, crickets, millipedes, centipedes, daddy longlegs, spiders, and more. Many snacked on bacteria and fungi growing on the guano. Others snacked on the guano itself, and still others ate the snackers.

"Why are many of the critters white?" asked Baby Bat.

"They're white because they never leave the cave," said Pluribus. "Many are blind, too. Here in the dark, they don't need colors to hide from other animals or eyes to see."

A nearby stream held more ghostly creatures. Pluribus rippled the cold water with his paw. A cavefish swam over, expecting to find a water critter to eat.

At the stream's bottom, the flashlight lit up a cave crayfish waving long antennae, and a blind salamander resting on a rock.

"Do the water critters get food from bats, too?" asked the pup.

"They sure do," said Pluribus. "Rain seeps into the cave and washes the guano into the stream. The guano feeds the tiniest animals, and they become food for larger critters."

"Wow, I had no idea that so many animals depend on us for food!" exclaimed Baby Bat.

"Speaking of food," said Pluribus, "I haven't eaten yet tonight. Like you bats, I leave the cave to find food, but I eat berries, nuts, and seeds."

Pluribus took Baby Bat back to the nursery. The two hugged goodbye and promised to explore together again. Then Pluribus was off to fill his stomach, and perhaps find another shiny treasure.

As Baby Bat settled into his usual spot, he thought about all the cave critters that depended on bats. He started flapping his wings—faster and faster.

Maybe I could go hunting with mom, he thought. *She'd be there to protect me. It's not like I have to leave the cave forever.*

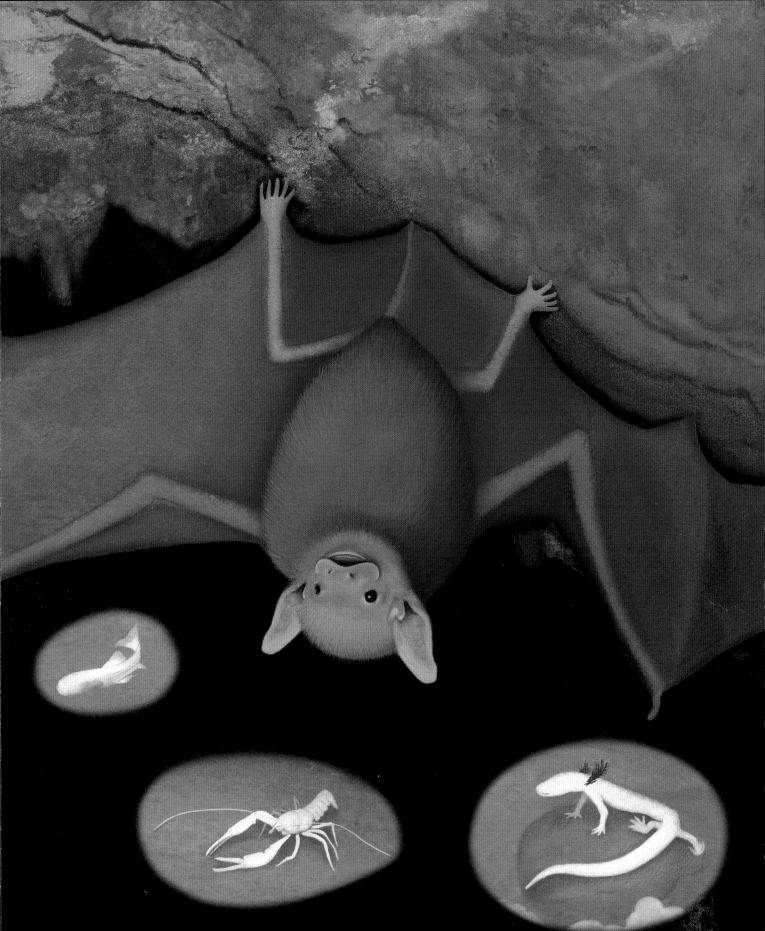

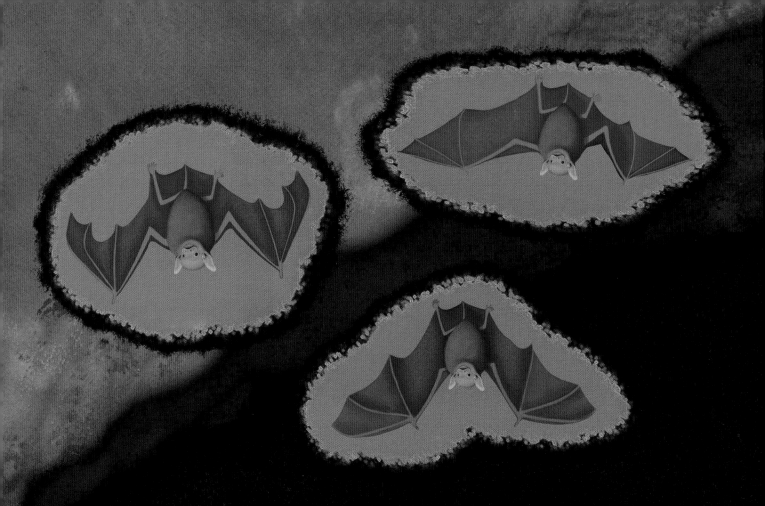

Mom soon returned, and Baby Bat snuggled with her, drinking warm milk. For the first time, he realized that his mom needed to eat insects to make milk for him.

"Mom, I practiced flapping my wings tonight," he said. "And you know what? I think I'm ready to go hunting with you."

His mom hugged him tight. Her Baby Bat was

For Creative Minds

Life in Cave Zones

Caves come in all different shapes, depths, sizes, and lengths. But they are all dark holes or tunnels in rocks or, in some cases, soil.

A cave's entrance can be very small or it can be big enough for humans and other large animals to walk easily in and out. Some entrances are narrow cracks in rocks that go into the rock or down into the ground. Depending on the size of the cave, there can be more than one entrance.

Natural sunlight in the cave's *entrance zone* lets some plants grow.

Going deeper into the cave, the *twilight zone* is where the sunlight turns into darkness. It is named after twilight—the time of day when sunlight turns to darkness. Animals that live in cave entrances and twilight zones travel out of the cave for food. So do bats and packrats, which live in either twilight or dark zones.

The *dark zone* receives no sunlight at all. Animals that live in the dark zone have special adaptations to help them move around without any light. They might not even have eyes because there isn't any light to see. They may have long antennae to feel their way. Food is carried to them by underground water, wind, or in the bat guano (poop).

What lives in which cave zone? There are two answers for each zone. Answers are upside down, below.

cave cricket

bird

blind salamander

cavefish

cave salamander

fern (plant)

Answers: entrance—bird, fern (plant); twilight—cave cricket (brown), cave salamander; dark—cavefish, blind salamander

Rock Formations

Some of the most beautiful and interesting features of caves are rock formations that either hang down from the cave ceiling or grow up from the cave floor. Smaller stalactites and stalagmites take hundreds to thousands of years to grow, while really large formations take hundreds of thousands of years.

 Stalactites hang "tight" from the cave's ceiling.

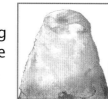 Stalagmites grow "mightily" from the cave floor up.

 When stalagmites and stalactites grow together, they form a column.

Cave Habitats

A habitat is where something lives—where it can meet all of its basic needs. Living things interact with each other and the non-living things in that same habitat. There are many different types of habitats all over the world. Deep caves open into another habitat, like a desert, forest, or even ocean. Some animals move in and out of more than one habitat daily or seasonally.

Living things rely on non-living things in their habitat: rocks or soil, water, air, and climate.

Plants need sunlight, water, nutrients in which to grow, and a way for seeds to move (disperse).

Animals need food, water, oxygen to breathe, and a safe space for shelter and to give birth to their young.

| 1 | Are these things living or non-living? |

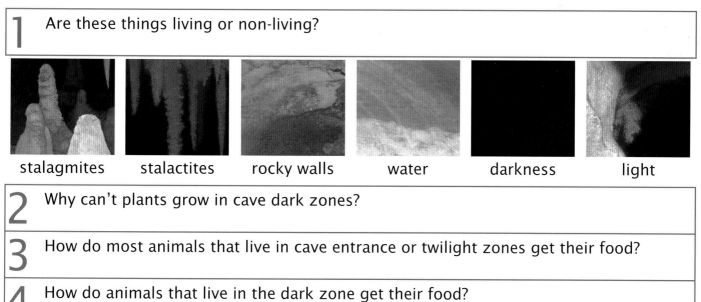

stalagmites   stalactites   rocky walls   water   darkness   light

| 2 | Why can't plants grow in cave dark zones? |

| 3 | How do most animals that live in cave entrance or twilight zones get their food? |

| 4 | How do animals that live in the dark zone get their food? |

Answers or possible answers: 1) They are all non-living. 2) Plants need sunlight to grow and there is no light in the dark zones. 3) They go out of the cave to get food. 4) They rely on the droppings of animals that eat outside the cave, the bodies of dead animals, and food carried into the cave by water and wind.

Hands On: Bat Echolocation

Imagine having to find your way around in the dark every night—without any lights to help you see. Many animals rest during the day and are active at night (nocturnal). Animals that live deep in caves survive with no light at all. These animals have special body parts and senses to help them "see" in the dark. Some animals use the sense of touch (whiskers or antennae) to be able to move in the dark. Some have eyes that are very large to absorb as much light as they can—even in the darkness. Others use their sense of sound. Most bats use something called

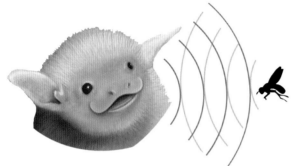

echolocation to help them "see" in the dark. They locate objects (insects to catch or trees to avoid) by listening to echoes or sound waves bouncing back at them.

Bats make high-pitched noises with their noses or mouths. The noises are so high pitched that we can't hear them (like a dog whistle). These sounds bounce off objects around them and back to the bats— echoes. Bats have very large ears to help them trap these echoes. Not only do the echoes tell bats where insects are, but their size! By "seeing" with these sounds, bats can catch insects in the air and can avoid flying into things.

To better understand sound waves, fill a large container or tub with water. Let the water settle so that it is very still. Now drop in a coin or small object. Watch the waves that travel out from the point where the object enters the water. Can you see the waves moving through the water? Sound makes waves too. Although we can't see sound waves with our eyes, we can hear them.

Do you think you could find an insect in the dark just by listening? Our sense of hearing is not as well developed as a bat's, but we still can sense location with hearing. Close your eyes and focus on the sounds around you. What do you hear? Can you tell where the sounds are coming from?

Bat and Bug

With three or more people, blindfold one person. That person is the "bat." Other people are either trees or bugs.

Similar to the game "Marco Polo" often played in a pool, the bat is "it" and calls out "bat."

The others must respond by saying "tree" or "bug."

The bat has to try to catch a bug without running into a tree.

The bugs can move but trees cannot.

Take turns being the bat, tree, and bug.

Is it easy to find your way around by sound?

Would you rather "see" with your eyes or your ears?

Compare and Contrast: Bats, Birds, & Humans

Like humans, bats are mammals. But unlike us, bats can fly. In fact, they are the only mammals that fly. Most birds fly too.

There are almost 1,100 species (different types) of bats and around 10,000 species of birds. This story is about a gray myotis, an endangered species. Thousands of these female bats gather in certain caves to raise their pups. Some of the other types of bats that gather in large numbers in caves to raise their young include the Mexican free-tailed bat, cave myotis, lesser long-nosed bat, and the southeastern myotis. Go to the book's online activities to see photos.

Bat hands have five digits—just as we have five fingers. But bats have a thick skin covering their "fingers," turning their "hands" into wings. Birds have three digits in their wings.

Bats are born alive and drink milk from their mothers, just like human babies. Birds hatch from eggs.

Bats sleep during the day and are awake at night (nocturnal). Most birds and humans are awake during the day and sleep at night (diurnal). Bats sleep upside down in trees, caves, mines, under bridges, or even in bat houses. Most humans sleep in beds, and birds sleep in nests, trees, or bushes.

Most bats use echolocation and eyes to see. Humans and birds see only with their eyes.

Bats and humans have hair (fur is hair), and birds have feathers.

Bats and humans have teeth but birds have beaks.

Are Bats Good or Bad?

Sometimes movies or stories make bats sound scary, bad, or dangerous. After learning about bat behaviors, you decide . . . are bats good or bad?

Bats eat lots of crop-eating insects, saving millions of dollars around the world in pesticides.

👍 or 👎

Some farmers use bat guano as fertilizer for their fields.

Many fruit-eating bats spread plant seeds. If you enjoy eating bananas, pineapples, mangos, dates, and figs, you can thank a bat for spreading those seeds.

Some bats pollinate flowers and plants. In fact, some types of cactus and agave rely on specific bats for pollination. If something happens to those bats, the plants won't survive either. Next time you use an agave-based lotion for a sunburn, you can thank a bat!

GRAYSLAKE PUBLIC LIBRARY
100 Library Lane
Grayslake, IL 60030

To my family, the wonders of my life. Many thanks to Rob Mies, Director of the Organization for Bat Conservation, for answering my many questions about bats—JH

While doing research for the illustrations, I drove to the mountains of Pennsylvania, flew to the desert of New Mexico, and circled back to the Charles River of Boston, MA. I would especially like to thank Jennifer Brumbaugh of Lincoln Caverns and Whispering Rocks for giving me a tour of their caves and a view of their hibernating bats; the NPS rangers and staff of Carlsbad Caverns for answering a million of my questions; Professor Thomas Kunz of The Center for Ecology and Conservation Biology at Boston University for welcoming me into the Kunz Bat Lab and allowing me to study his bats 'up close and personal'; and—as always—my loving, supportive family for cheering me ever onward to my next adventure—SB

Thanks to Sue Barnard, Founder of Basically Bats Wildlife Conservation Society and author of Bats In Captivity, for reviewing the bat information; and to Dale L. Pate, Cave & Karst Program Coordinator, Geologic Resources Division—National Park Service, and Kriste Lindberg, Chairman of the Environmental Education Committee of the National Speleological Society, for reviewing the accuracy of the cave-related information in this book.

Library of Congress Cataloging-in-Publication Data

Halfmann, Janet.
  Home in the cave / by Janet Halfmann ; illustrated by Shennen Bersani.
      p. cm.
  ISBN 978-1-60718-522-2 (hardcover) -- ISBN 978-1-60718-531-4 (pbk.) -- ISBN 978-1-60718-540-6 (english ebook) -- ISBN 978-1-60718-549-9 (spanish ebook) 1. Bats--Juvenile literature. 2. Cave animals--Juvenile literature. I. Bersani, Shennen, ill. II. Title.
  QL737.C5H335 2012
  599.4--dc23
                                     2011040284

Also available as eBooks featuring auto-flip, auto-read, 3D-page-curling, and selectable English and Spanish text and audio
Interest level: 004-009 Grade level: P-4 Lexile® Level: 750 Lexile® Code: AD
Curriculum keywords: adaptations, anthropomorphic, compare/contrast, food web, get food/water, habitat, interconnectedness, landforms, life science: general, living/non-living

Manufactured in China, December, 2011
This product conforms to CPSIA 2008
First Printing
Published by Sylvan Dell Publishing
Mt. Pleasant, SC 29464